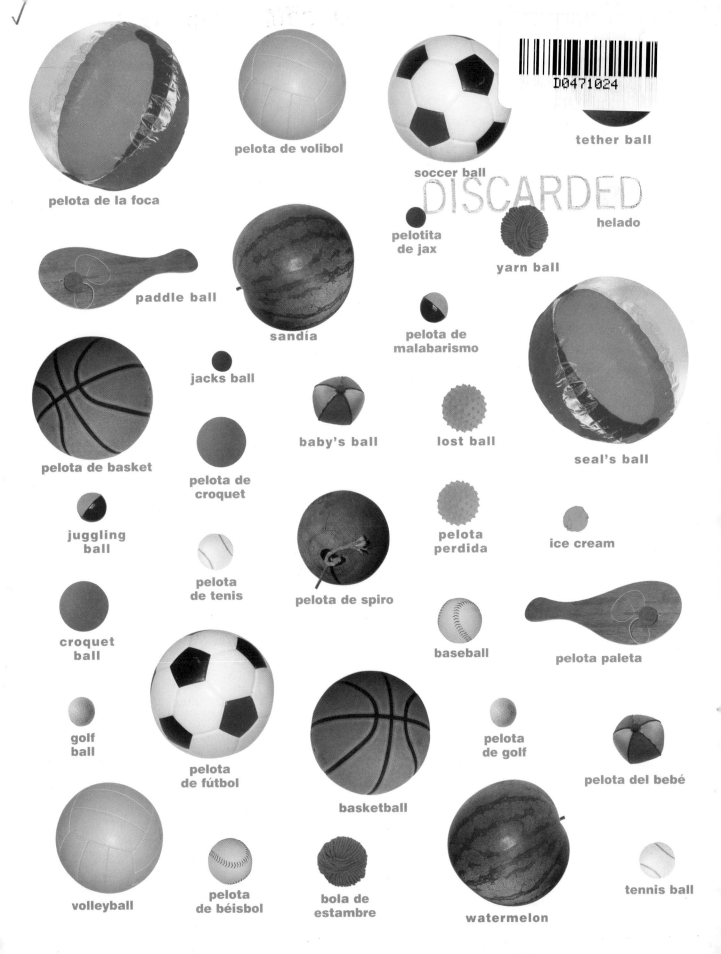

pelota de volibol

soccer ball

tether ball

pelota de la foca

DISCARDED

helado

pelotita
de jax

yarn ball

paddle ball

sandía

pelota de
malabarismo

jacks ball

baby's ball

lost ball

seal's ball

pelota de basket

pelota de
croquet

juggling
ball

pelota
perdida

ice cream

pelota
de tenis

pelota de spiro

croquet
ball

pelota de spiro

baseball

pelota paleta

golf
ball

pelota
de fútbol

pelota
de golf

pelota del bebé

basketball

volleyball

pelota
de béisbol

bola de
estambre

watermelon

tennis ball

D0471024

The Lost Ball

La pelota perdida

By Lynn Reiser

Translated by M. J. Infante

Greenwillow Books
An Imprint of HarperCollinsPublishers

rayo

"Of course . . ."
to Susan and Ava, with love

Thanks to
Rolena Adorno, Fernanda Macchi,
Graziella de Solodow, and Joseph B. Solodow
for their thoughtful and meticulous attention to finding
exactly the right Spanish words,

and to Phyllis Larkin for her consistent and loving concern

Rayo is an imprint of HarperCollins Publishers, Inc.

Black line, watercolors, and photographs were used to prepare the full-color art.
The text type is Swiss 721 Black.

Library of Congress Cataloging-in-Publication Data: Reiser, Lynn. The lost ball / La pelota
perdida / by Lynn Reiser ; Spanish translation by M.J. Infante.   p.   cm.
"Greenwillow Books." Summary: English-speaking Richard and Spanish-speaking
Ricardo and their dogs walk through the park, each looking for his lost ball.
ISBN 0-06-029763-8 (trade). ISBN 0-06-029764-6 (lib. bdg.)
[1. Balls (Sporting goods)—Fiction. 2. Spanish language materials—
Bilingual.] I. Title: La pelota perdida.   II. Infante, M.J.   III.
Title. PZ73.R416 2002   [E]—dc21   2001033272

1 2 3 4 5 6 7 8 9 10
First Edition

**Today
is a good day
to play ball
in the park,
Comet.**

**Hoy
es un lindo día
para jugar
a la pelota
en el parque,
Cometa.**

Catch, Comet!

**Come,
Comet.
Come!**

¡Busca, Cometa!

GUAU
GUAU

**Ven,
Cometa.
¡Ven!**

Oh, Comet!
This is not
our ball.

Whose ball
is this?

¡Ah, Cometa!
Esta no es
nuestra pelota.

¿De quién es
esta pelota?

Let's go find the owner of this ball!

¡Vamos
a buscar
al dueño
de esta
pelota!

**Is this
your ball?**

**No,
our ball is
a tennis ball.**

¿Es ésta
tu pelota?

No,
nuestra pelota es
una pelota de basket.

**Is this
your ball?**

**No,
our ball is
a baseball.**

¿Es ésta tu pelota?

No, nuestra pelota es una pelota de fútbol.

Is this your ball?

No, our ball is a golf ball.

**¿Es ésta
tu pelota?**

*No,
nuestra pelota es
una pelota de volibol.*

Look, Comet!
Ice cream!
Today
is a good day
to eat ice cream
in the park!

Thank you.

¡Mira, Cometa!
¡Helado!
¡Hoy
es un lindo día
para tomar helado
en el parque!

Gracias.

¡Pero
tenemos que encontrar
nuestra pelota
y al dueño
de esta pelota!

But
we must find
our ball
and the owner
of this ball!

¿Es ésta
tu pelota?

No,
nuestra pelota es
una pelota de golf.

**Is this
your ball?**

**No,
our ball is
a volleyball.**

**¿Es ésta
tu pelota?**

**No,
nuestra pelota es
una pelota de béisbol.**

**Is this
your ball?**

*No,
our ball is
a soccer ball.*

¿Es ésta
tu pelota?

No,
nuestra pelota es
una pelota de tenis.

**Is this
your ball?**

**No,
our ball is
a basketball.**

¡Ah,
Cometa!
Encontramos
una pelota de basket
y
una pelota de fútbol
y
una pelota de volibol.

Y encontramos
una pelota de golf
y
una pelota de béisbol
y
una pelota de tenis.

Pero
no encontramos
la pelota nuestra.

Oh,
Comet!
We found
a basketball
and
a soccer ball
and
a volleyball.

And we found
a golf ball
and
a baseball
and
a tennis ball.

But
we did not find
our ball.

¡Mira, Cometa!   **Look, Comet!**

**¡Esta es
nuestra
pelota perdida!**   **That is
our
lost ball!**

¡Qué
buen perrito!

What a
good dog!

Mi perro
se llama
Cometa.

My dog's
name is
Comet.

Yo me llamo
Ricardo.

My name is
Richard.

Good-bye, Ricardo.
Adiós, Richard.
Good-bye, Cometa.
Adiós, Comet.
See you tomorrow!
¡Hasta mañana!

¡Adiós! Good-bye!

¡GUAU!

BARK!

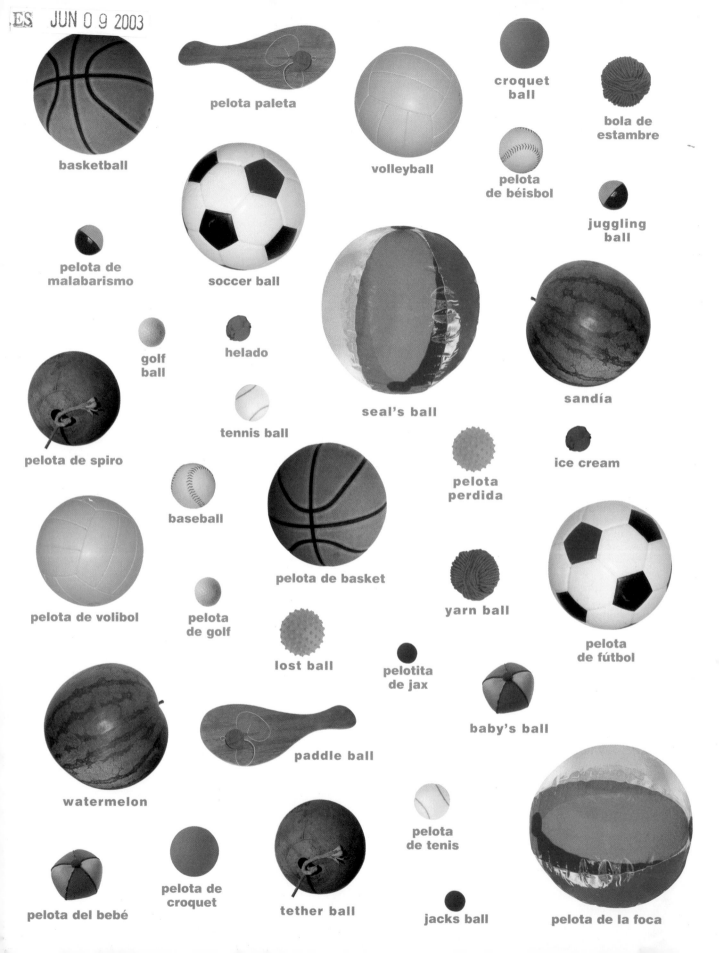

basketball

pelota paleta

volleyball

croquet ball

bola de estambre

pelota de béisbol

juggling ball

pelota de malabarismo

soccer ball

golf ball

helado

seal's ball

sandía

pelota de spiro

tennis ball

ice cream

pelota perdida

baseball

pelota de basket

pelota de volibol

pelota de golf

lost ball

pelotita de jax

yarn ball

pelota de fútbol

baby's ball

watermelon

paddle ball

pelota del bebé

pelota de croquet

tether ball

pelota de tenis

jacks ball

pelota de la foca